CHILDREN'S DEPT.

Modern Curriculum Press
BEGINNING
TO
READ
Series

CIRCUS FUN

Margaret Hillert

Illustrated by ELAINE RAPHAEL

THOMAS JEFFERSON LIBRARY SYSTEM
214 Adams Street
Jefferson City, Missouri 65101

MODERN CURRICULUM PRESS
Cleveland • Toronto

Copyright © 1969, by Modern Curriculum Press, Inc. Original copyright © 1969, by Follett Publishing Company, a division of Follett Corporation. All rights reserved. No part of this book may be reproduced in any form without written permission from the publisher.
Manufactured in the United States of America.

ISBN 0-8136-5511-0 Paperback
ISBN 0-8136-5011-9 Hardbound

5 6 7 8 9 10 88 87

CIRCUS FUN

Oh, Father, look, look.
Here is something funny.
I want to go to it.

CIRCUS
TODAY!

Father said, "Come, come.
We can go.
Run, run, run."

I see it.

Here it is.

We go in here.

Here is something big.

Big, big, big.

It can work.

It can help.

See it make something go up.

Something red and blue and yellow.

Oh, my.

We want to go in.

Here we go, Father.

Up, here, up here.

Help me go up.

I see something.
I want something.
I want a red one.

Oh, look, look.

One little one.

Two big ones.

See the blue ball.

The little one can play ball.

See something funny.
It can go up.
It can come down.
Up and down.
Up and down.

Oh, oh, oh.

Look up here.

Look up and up and up.

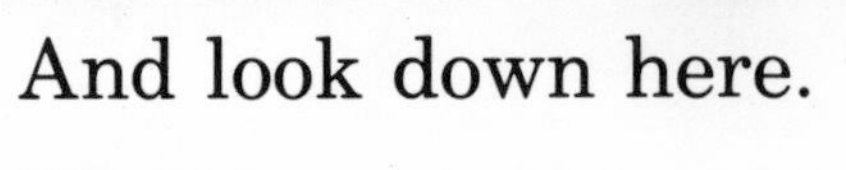
And look down here.

Here is something big.

It is yellow.

It wants to jump and play.

Here is a funny one.

I see three balls.

Red, yellow, and blue balls.

Oh, oh.

Where is the red ball?

Where is the yellow ball?

Where is the blue ball?

Here is one.

Here is one.

And — here is one.

See my funny car.
Come into my funny car.
We can go away in it.
Away, away, away.

Look here.
See the big father.
See the big mother.
See the little baby.

You can go up.
I can help you go up.
Up you go.

Oh, Father, Father.

See me.

See me.

It is fun up here.

3 1331 00249 1753

Down.

Down.

Down I come.

Mother, Mother.

Look here.

Here is something for you.

And here is a cookie for you.
Cookies for you and Father.

Modern Curriculum Press Beginning-To-Read Books

Margaret Hillert, author of several books in the MCP Beginning-To-Read Series, is a writer, poet, and teacher.

CIRCUS FUN

A boy and his father have an eventful and exciting day at the circus, told in 50 preprimer words.

Word List

6 oh
father
look
here
is
something
funny
I
want (s)
to
go
it
8 said
come
we
can
run
9 see
in
10 big
work
help
11 make
up
red
and
blue
yellow
my
12 me
13 a
one (s)
14 little
two
the
ball (s)
play
15 down
18 jump
19 three
20 where
22 car
into
away
23 mother
baby
24 you
25 fun
28 for
29 cookie (s)